The Father of Octopus Wrestling
and other small fictions

THE FATHER OF OCTOPUS WRESTLING

AND OTHER SMALL FICTIONS

FRANKIE McMILLAN

CANTERBURY UNIVERSITY PRESS

UNIVERSITY OF
CANTERBURY
Te Whare Wānanga o Waitaha
CHRISTCHURCH NEW ZEALAND

First published in 2019 by
CANTERBURY UNIVERSITY PRESS
University of Canterbury
Private Bag 4800, Christchurch
NEW ZEALAND
www.canterbury.ac.nz/engage/cup

ISBN 978-1-98-850312-7

A catalogue record for this book is available from the
National Library of New Zealand.

Editor: Emma Neale
Art direction: Aaron Beehre
Publication design: Aaron Beehre
Cover illustration: Irenie Howe
Printed at Ilam Press by Aaron Beehre and Gabriel van Schouten

Published with the support of Creative New Zealand

ARTS COUNCIL OF NEW ZEALAND TOI AOTEAROA

Contents

The happy eggs from Podomosky

Jesus and the ostriches

The man who saved the world gives
the teachings of the trolley bus

THE FATHER OF OCTOPUS WRESTLING

Seven starts to the man who loved trees

1.

Jazz Novitz is my name. I'm the hitchhiker who was kidnapped, forced to live in a tree. People remember my name, what with all the Zs. My mother said when she came to New Zealand she kept on seeing Zs. Menz haircuts, Split Enz, Trendz furniture etc., so when she got pregnant with me she used all the Zs she could. I can't get a job using my real name. I've given up on that.

The worst thing is when, in a crowded supermarket or on the bus, I feel a light touch on the arm. I turn around to face a wide-eyed stranger, *uh oh, here we go again.* Women particularly want to hear my story. They think maybe there's a special way of talking to a kidnapper or a murderer so that they manage to get away unharmed. They say I must have been cool-headed to carry out what I did and sometimes I let them think all these things because then nothing more is expected of me. I don't have to become anybody, don't have to prove myself. I can just sit here, peacefully, gaze out onto the lawn.

The wind has blown more leaves down from the neighbour's tree. Every day I rake them up, bag them in black plastic bags to compost and every day new leaves fall. I have to tell myself there's as many leaves as there are stories. And what

. . .

people really want to hear is what happens between the gaps, about the falling, and if I can find the plain language for that then maybe I can begin. My name is Jazz Novitz. He carried a gun and knew everything there was to know about trees.

2.

Monday, it's raining hard and you're stuck in a tree hut with a stranger. Below, the river breaks its banks, flooding the paddocks. You give the girl a towel to dry her hair but she leaves it on the stretcher. So then you light up the gas cooker and she complains the fumes are making her sick. You regret stopping to give her a lift, regret having a toke up there when you should have been keeping your eye on the rising ford. So now you know it's true; trouble always comes in threes. First, the cabbage trees, dropping their leaves, turning black from some virus, then the new plantings getting washed away … no matter how fast you work you're never going to keep pace with the bloody erosion and now there's a sick girl in your hut.

3.

He was lonely, he must have seen me at the side of the road and thought that somehow I would save him.

4.

For a while the tree hut was empty. Magpies nested on the roof, the branches pressed in on the two high windows. When the wind blew, the rachet on the pulley system creaked and dislodged feathers fluttered in the air. Above the roar of the river the sound of a vehicle came closer. It spluttered through the ford then came to a shuddering halt by the oak tree. A man and a girl got out. Though there was no other house in sight she asked for a bathroom. 'Bathroom?' said the man. The girl pointed to a shed in the distance, light catching on the corrugated roof. The man continued to pull out provisions from the van. It took him a while to realize what she was saying. 'Go behind a tree,' he said. He hauled out a shovel to give to her. The blade caught on the sacking and when he yanked on it an object wrapped in yellow cloth shot out onto the ground. They both stared at the metal barrel poking from the cloth. 'Heck, it's not what you think,' said the man.

5.

The police report records the dates, February 16th – February 23rd; summary of facts; previous conviction list; photographs of the tree hut, the property, the van; the distance in kilometres from the hut to the Main North road but nothing about the way the tree hut swayed in the wind; the sudden bird shit falling past the window; Lloyd's greyish white tooth; his scraggly pony tail; the long nights and the low hiss of the Tilley lamp; heavy slam of the trap door; the rising vomit in my throat; the scream and scrape of magpie claws on the roof and in the distance an early morning tractor back-firing; Lloyd running over the paddock, even as he was shot, running and being shot and brought down, blood from his head and a voice – it must have been mine – *do you have to keep shooting him?*

· · ·

6.

I told Lloyd I was sniffing leaves. I had my head out the
little window and I said I loved the smell of leaves after rain.
Lloyd looked pleased. 'There's a name for that.' He took my
arm and led me away from the window. 'You remember the
name I told you?' I didn't. But I'd gotten away with it, I'd
pushed the window open and seen the rope ladder, the van
and beyond the swollen river to the road.

I lay back on the camp stretcher looking up at the damp
washing drying overhead. Lloyd sat on his chair bending
a piece of wire with pliers. 'Petrichor,' he announced. His
mouth opened wide. 'Petrichor ... smell of leaves and dry
grass after rain.' Outside the wind picked up, knocking a
branch against the plywood walls. Lloyd looked up. 'So what
did I say?'

I closed my eyes. I was thinking how clever a leaf could be.
How it knew when rain was coming, how it knew when to
burst from a bud, the right moment to fall from the tree.

7.

Looking after trees is a lot easier than looking after people.
You tend to their wounds, brace and cable, talk nicely to
them and the next day those trees are just where you left
them. *Jazz*. That was the one who almost got away.

The father of octopus wrestling

My father sleepwalks, his arms outstretched as if to strangle
someone. My mother doesn't bother getting up for him
now. Before bedtime she clears the stairway of any shoes or
dropped items that might trip him and that is that.

My father is noisiest in the bathroom. *Roll up! Roll up!* he
cries. He turns on the bath taps. The overhead shower. Water
pours from the sink.

My mother says she's had it with him. She says there's
a medical name for a broken heart – Takotsubo
cardiomyopathy. A Japanese surgeon named it after he saw
the broken heart's resemblance to an octopus trap.

My father is naked in the bath. He starts wrestling with an
invisible opponent.

My mother buys a big aquarium tank. At the bottom is
a little city of ceramic houses, bubbles rising from the
chimney. She lowers my father feet first into the cool water.
Underwater his head looks enormous.

My father presses his beaky lips to the sides of the glass.

My mother cries. She wishes she had three hearts instead of
one – that way they could start all over again.

The honking of ducks

The thing to do with a secret is to swallow it, and just as
you're not bothered by thoughts of a plum's progress through
your intestinal tract, neither will you think of your sister
running hand in hand with a strange man to the river bank
and when your sister goes missing you will have to borrow
words to explain why you never told and when the police
say who put those words into your mouth you will think
only of the loveliness of weeping willows, the *ssshhh* sweep of
fronds over the sandy bank, all the fun you will have when
your sister sets up house under water and you have to swim
through the clefts in rocks holding your breath against the
squeeze. And when you come up for air you will stand firm
upon your promise and not allude, refer to, speak or even
write about your sister's sweet underwater life but instead
speak mysteriously about the mammalian reflex; how humans
can survive in freezing water for longer than expected.

Meanwhile you wait with your mother on the river bank.
She says she will thrash you to get the truth out if she has to,
but the secret has long turned to pip, to gravel, to stone.

'Listen to the ducks, Mama,' you say trailing your hand
through the water.

The bride from Clarry's Vineyard

So we're just finishing up the wedding cakes when I remember
we haven't placed the little bride and bridegroom on the top
of the one for Clarry's Vineyard and I look at the order just
to check it's not two of the same; two brides in white or two
grooms in black which is becoming more common these days
and Johnny wipes his hands on his apron and says, we've got
to get more ventilation in here, the iced flowers aren't looking
too perky and I point to the order and say, who took this
order and Johnny says what's wrong with it and I say there's
something missing, that's what wrong and Johnny shuffles
forward, back hunched as a hamster and stares at the paper
for so long, pity takes hold and I say, look here there's only
one figurine put down for the top tier of the cake … *so who's
she going to marry, huh?* And we hold the order up to the light
from the window but there's nothing ticked there and Johnny
says maybe there's not supposed to be another figure and now
my kindness towards Johnny, after working in the bakery for
twenty-five years, my kindness starts to harden like a ball of
sugar at three forty Fahrenheit and I bark at him, how can
that be, what are you trying to say and I push past him to the
decoration drawers and pull out a handful of plastic brides and
bridegrooms and I say, *sort it, Johnny.*

But even as I'm banging the drawers shut and even as he
bends down to wipe the sweat off his forehead I know, just as

. . .

I know about climate warming, and infertility, and too much plastic in the ocean, and the rising divorce rate, I know this bride is going to walk through Clarry's Vineyard and before the priest she'll put her own ring on her own finger and this is just the beginning of other brides, all over the country walking alone on their wedding day and what I'm going to do with all the extra plastic bridegrooms in the drawer, I don't know.

How we occupy ourselves

Though we don't do much together like other families, don't go on holidays and stuff because Papa lives down by the river in half the house and we stay with Mama in the other half on the flat, we still go to Sunday dinner at my grandmother's house and though Mama and Papa bicker over the table there's things they agree on still, like the terrible government and the terrible war in Afghanistan and us kids sit and listen to their voices rumbling on over our heads and sometimes a good story will pop out like a shucked pea and it might be a story exactly the same as every other story to roll across the table but sometimes it's a story we've never heard before like why Mama ran off with Geordie Lovelace and why it was that Papa bought a gun.

Because all Papa wanted to do was scare the living daylights out of Geordie Lovelace, let him know there was consequences to what he did. But Papa got the wrong motel room and inside was a visiting optometrist with glasses and eye charts laid out on the bed who at the sight of Papa wielding a gun, ran into the bathroom. And Papa hammered on the door saying he was sorry, so very sorry, there'd been a terrible mistake but already the optometrist was phoning the police and Papa panicked and he says he don't know why but he grabbed a pair of spectacles from the bed and walked slowly as he could with them on, past the reception and out to his car.

. . .

This is when Mama takes over the story. She says she and Geordie are lying by the beachside pool when the phone rings and her boyfriend says don't answer that but Mama says, I have to, it might be something's happened to one of the kids and she answers the phone to hear Papa has crashed his car, his head is bleeding, glass in his face, he needs her, *honey, come straightaway.*

So some things go from bad to worse but what us kids don't understand is why can't they go back from worse to bad. It was only a little bit of fighting and bitching between them and Mama still drove out to rescue Papa but she never stayed long and soon after that Papa returned with a chainsaw and ripped the house clean down the middle. Takes Papa all week to drag half a house down to the river bank but he says he can't see any other man putting up his hand for the job. And us kids and even Grandmother know not to ask the whereabouts of Geordie Lovelace. Instead our parents, full of chicken and gravy and Grandmother's roly poly pudding, smile at us kids and say how lucky we are, all of us alive with roofs over our heads and telling each other stories and if this is what folks didn't do on a holiday then they sure as hell didn't know what they did do.

The geography of a father

There were landscapes and landscapes. They drove through
County Clare towards the Burren; she expected to feel
uplifted, to gaze in awe at the towering limestone cliffs, the
field of stones, to get weepy at 'The Road of the Dishes'.
When she was little her grandmother had told her stories and
she'd imagined white pudding bowls that stretched for miles.

She didn't like the Burren. The relentless grey, the everywhere
karst and stone and boulder and nothing, not even a tree
moving. It was like her childhood home on Sundays.
Her father sleeping in the spare room – the pearl button
accordion by his bed, empty of wind.

'Can't we go back?' she asked but the journey was on their
list, it was ancestral land, it had to be ticked off. Sometimes
the only way was through. She'd read that somewhere; you
just had to grit your teeth, suck it up, keep going.

Much later she'd meet others who'd been inspired by the
Burren. They'd climbed the cliffs, written screeds of poetry,
painted the grikes and clints, the limestone pavement, they
were *blown away* by the Burren. But for now she was in that
in-between place, the same place she'd been in as a child.
When all was said and done and the shouting died down she
was supposed to love him. But she didn't love her father and

. . .

it gave rise to a sadness and an awful longing in her and a great capacity to lie.

'The Burren was awesome,' she'd later say, staring into her plate, 'truly awesome.'

Wrestling with the octopus

An octopus can wrestle the life out of you, hands down.

$((((\quad))))$

It swaggers, cartoon-style into your life; open-armed,
thuggish, a grab bag of wants and wins and big-hearted
laughter. Say 'No' to the octopus, say, 'Hang on there,
buddy,' say, 'Not one step further,' say, 'I got a knife on me,'
and the octopus goes all Houdini. Disappears in a sulk.
Comes back smooth. A Marlboro hanging from its beaky mouth.

And that one dominant eye? It swivels around, a gelatinous
orb, fixes you with such longing.

Call the octopus a squid. A cephalopodic old fart. Tell the
octopus you don't want to wrestle. Shout it out. 'I'm only me
with two arms. How can I apply a full nelson? A crotch hold
when *you've* got eight crotches?' $((((\quad))))$

Find more excuses.

Tell the octopus you've fallen on hard times. Show the
octopus the bits of coral stuck in your knees, wedged
between your toes, splintered in your teeth. Then watch the
octopus play the piano, its limbs gliding over the keys as it
sings the blues for you.

. . .

Know the octopus will never quit asking. Even when the octopus is slumped in the weeds, his grey hoodie pulled low, you know he's still asking.

26   Begin to think *play fight*. Roly-poly, tumble and fun. Begin again. Begin eight times. An octopus can wrestle the life out of you, hands down. Say it.

That's enough about the octopus. I bet the octopus has its own story. I bet someone else will come along pretty soon and wrestle with the octopus.

((((   ))))

There's no slowing down at Anne Frank's house

We hurry up the steep stairs of the canal house. It's nearly closing time and there are others behind us, a queue that stretches out into the Amsterdam night. You say, 'Stay close to me,' and I clutch the back of your jacket as we edge through corridors and up another flight of rickety stairs. And then we're in Anne Frank's bedroom, the wallpaper dotted with torn off pictures of film stars and faded royalty but it's the postcard titled *The Chimpanzee's Tea Party!* that makes me stop. I stare at the chimpanzees from the Berlin Zoo; they sit at a table, two with paws over their mouths as if about to whisper something. I think of Anne slowly and carefully pasting the back of the postcard, positioning it on the wall next to Ginger Rogers.

Downstairs we hear heavy footfalls on the stairs. 'Keep moving,' you urge, as the throng of people pushes us forward into the next room. I tell you I want to slow down. I tell you I want to go back. 'Why are we always rushing?' I say.

You frown. You explain as if I'm a child. 'Nobody goes back, honey,' you say, 'there's only one way out of here.'

A good match

My husband appears at the studio door. I glance at him over the easel. It's the third time he's changed his shirt. 'Does this look okay?' he says. He wears green jeans and a white T-shirt with black letters small as broken spider legs. 'It's better,' I say. 'Better than before.'

Outside it is quiet. The neighbours are sleeping off hangovers, kids' bikes sprawled in the yard, the air still fuggy with wine and charred meat. My husband says they had a good time last night, he heard them singing; grandmothers, uncles, aunts, small kids. He pulls his T-shirt out from his trousers. 'Better out or in?'

I want to be kind. To say whatever he wears he is the most handsome man on the street. But always a small hurt comes if I lie. 'Does an elephant have to work hard at being an elephant?' I say. He shrugs. Pulls his white T-shirt loose over his belly. 'I'm off,' he says. 'You remember where I'm going?'

He is going to meet his woman friend, drink coffee and argue about God's existence. While he's gone the neighbours will rouse themselves. The old arguments will begin, someone will rake the yard, hose dog shit off the cobbles, grandmothers will find a patch of sun and raise their faces to the warmth. I will stand alone before a blank canvas. After a

. . .

while I'll go into my husband's room. Stare at the abandoned shirts thrown over the bed. Wonder again about what goes best, this or that, blue with green, him with me or her.

Road kill

After I split from my wife it took me a while to find a
job. The one I finally landed pulled me from my bed at
all hours, had me driving over the big marble mountain
and down to the city. There was a psych hospital there
and I delivered the bad cases. Girls who'd tried to string
themselves up from a tree, or jump from the Moraka bridge,
or run onto the road, right in front of a cattle truck. I had
a support buddy in the back of the van with them and
he'd be saying things like, 'Everything is gonna be all right.
You're safe now.' But those girls didn't want to be safe. They
bitched about how hard it was to kill themselves. It wasn't
fair they couldn't run out into the road, they said, wasn't fair
they couldn't stockpile their meds, razors or take any sort of
a rope where they were heading.

Sometimes I'd be driving over the winding pass, the
headlights flickering over the trees and a possum would dart
out across the road. I'd try and avoid it – those crazed, yellow
eyes caught in the glare, the bushy tail as if electrified.

Chrissake! my buddy would yell as the van began to swerve.
'It's only a possum.' What neither of us could understand
was how wound up the girls got if the possum was hit. Soon
as they heard the sickening thud as it went under the wheel
they'd begin screaming. *Stop the van!* They wanted to check

. . .

that the possum was dead and if so, they'd get all hysterical about giving it a proper burial. 'You can't just leave it there!' they'd cry. I had to promise them.

32   So that's how I arrived at the psych hospital – the patient in the back cradling a dead or broken animal. My buddy smoking out the window. Me doing a bit of explaining to the psych staff about the blood on my hands.

Doing the return trip back to Moraka, I could have flung the corpse into the scrub. Who would be there to see? Sometimes my buddy, eager to get home, would grab a tail and do just that. But I knew I'd had enough of broken promises in my life. When I got to the top of the mountain I'd always pull over. Grab a shovel and start chipping away at the rocky shale.

My buddy liked to stand there in the early morning sun, looking down the mountainside to the town below. And when he ground out his cigarette butt he'd begin talking but I was never sure whether it was about the possums or the girls. 'What's wrong with them?' he'd say. 'Why do they do that crazy shit?'

The hurry to dress

It's not easy to dress a chimpanzee in a frilly taffeta frock.
The zookeeper keeps up a constant chatter about pink iced
buns and how Matilda O is the prettiest girl and *my god, stay
still why don't you*, as he fastens the two little buttons on the
front and the chimpanzee squirms, bares its yellowed teeth
and screams.

This is how it happens every Friday at 2 p.m. in the Berlin
Zoo, no matter the weather, no matter if Hitler survives yet
another assassination attempt, no matter if a British bomb
blows the iron gates sky high and the air so thick with grey
no one notices the elephants lumbering out into the broken
street. It's as if dressing Matilda O is all the zookeeper can
keep in his head. That and the little table he lays with a red
gingham cloth, the thick china mugs, the dainty serviettes he
rolls and pokes through silver holders.

Evie Lu and Noddy have long since gone. Rumour has
it their chains were melted down for bullets, their organs
preserved and pickled for the Deutsches Museum but the
zookeeper laughs at these explanations. Evie Lu and Noddy
required more training; neither mastered drinking tea in a
leisurely fashion, neither could keep the mug at their lips
for long. Whereas Matilda O, once she had caught sight
of the pink iced buns, remembered the sequence perfectly.

. . .

She stood on her hind legs facing the audience. Waited for the zookeeper to pull back her chair. And when she sat, jibbering with excitement as the tea was poured, those in the front row couldn't help but notice how one of the little

buttons dangled loose from a thread on her pink frock. The zookeeper was obviously in a hurry, they said. The whole world was in a damn hurry.

THE HAIRY CHILD

Reading the signs

My father was going on again about Bozo, the signing chimp. How he had to pass his cage on his way to bagging up the elephant manure. How the chimp, locked up for something like ten years, would still hurry over to the bars and sign. *Key. Out. Hurry.*

I sat by my father's hospital bed looking into his dark upturned nostrils. The heat of that room and something about his nostrils was all mixed up in his ramblings about the chimp. I put a cold cloth on his forehead. 'About that chimp … did he come from the jungle?'

'What sort of question is that?' wheezed my father. He closed his eyes. I tried to read the numbers on the machine he was hooked up to. There was a red flashing light that came on every ten seconds but I didn't know if it was a good thing or a bad thing.

My father opened one eye, motioned me to come closer. 'Snatched from his mother …' he whispered. '… brought up like a human baby …'

'That was nothing to do with you, right?'

My father hauled himself up. His pyjama front stuck to his

. . .

trembling chest. 'I shoulda freed him.'

I straightened his collar. Reminded him of all the kind things he'd done for Bozo – poked an ice cream, a smoke, a live mouse through the bars. 'You go now,' he sighed.

Outside on the hospital lawn I looked up at his room. The nurse had wheeled him to the window. I waved, knowing that it was probably the last time I'd be seeing him but wanting the wave to convey all the love I had inside me, all the things I was wanting to do and all the things I was wanting to say but couldn't.

Cover up

I can't explain what it is to love a chimp and then have that chimp turn on you any more than I can explain about the breastfeeding. Of course I didn't feed Bozo in public, didn't whip up my blouse and let him have it, no mother did in those days. You excused yourself, is what you did, you went to the bathroom and sat on the toilet and it was no different with a chimp. And if in public his fingers were tearing at my buttons and people were staring, I'd hunch over and pretend it was something else. Pull loose a finger. Cry, 'Here's the church, here's the steeple, open the door' *cup his little paw over* 'here's all the people …'

I don't think it fooled anyone. There was always a damp tell-tale patch on my blouse.

40

Keeping Evie Lu quiet

While my father argues with the motel owner we play the quietest game I can think of: 'Where is your nose, Evie Lu? Point to your nose,' and she swings her hairy arm up to her face, points her finger to her flat chimp nose that always feels like putty under my fingers. I have my back to the car window and I have a leash around my sister's neck. Through the closed window I can hear my father's loud voice, not shouting, but raised like he's on stage giving a lecture to his psych students and he's telling the motel owner that Evie Lu is not a pet, she's a child, a family member and he will pay if the carpet is stained or if there's any breakages, that is standard policy wherever you go in the world and the motel owner in his blue shirt is almost levitating, he rises on the balls of his toes in his eagerness to explain the motel regulations and later my father will point this out to me. 'Body language,' he will say, 'did you notice that body language?' But that is later, a hundred kilometres later when we sneak into the Waterfront Motel, Evie Lu curled over my shoulders and my father flourishing the key at the motel door. It is not now, in a stiflingly hot car where boredom sets in, where my sister suddenly scurries over to the passenger window, the leash slipping, slipping from my sweaty hand, the sky opening up to her outraged scream.

The hairy child

Because my father is not really out to hurt my mother
and because the day is soon going to end and my bed is
too messed up to sleep in I climb the wardrobe and make
another bed in the trees. First I drag up a faded red quilt. It
has a few patches of Sellotape at the edge where the feathers
leak out. If I curl up on this small hard space I might just fit.
My legs of course are short. They are also covered in black
hair. My father says he has never seen such a hairy child. I
tell him my face is not covered in hair, or my ears, fingers
and toes, but he laughs. He says, 'What is this hairy girl
doing, sitting on top of the wardrobe?' My mother hears our
voices. 'Don't talk to him,' she says from the doorway.

I lie down, the sky so close if I sneezed it would rain. No one
can get me up in the highest branch. After a while I call out.
Yes, my mother says, she'll bring my dinner up to the top of
the wardrobe. A long time passes. The house is quiet. I stroke
my hairy legs. It's times like these I get anxious – wondering
about the next fight between my parents, wondering if the
tall tree of my childhood will stand firm in the storm.

When gorillas sleep

I never touched the gorilla, I say. I got better things to do.
Then the park ranger plonks his canvas bag on the table and
pulls out a tranquilliser gun and we all stare at the gun and
I know it will have my fingerprints all over it and then he's
saying, funny how you target the adolescent males, none
of the silverbacks are shot and I just about blurt out that's
just chance, that is, but I hold my tongue and I'm thinking
of fingerprints and even nose prints because each Ugandan
gorilla has got its own, nobody else like it. *Listen up!* The
park ranger bangs the table with his fist. A drop of sweat
runs down his forehead. You think we're going to sit here,
twiddle our thumbs while Rome burns? He leans forward,
tells me the whole conservation programme is under threat,
the government can pull its funding just like that and he's
not going to see his job go down the tubes. *Listen up!*

I never touched the gorilla, I say. And then he tells me to
think back to Lake Bunyonyi reserve yesterday afternoon and
what was I doing there? He knows I was there, he has proof.
Didn't I know there was cameras in the trees?

All the candelabra trees? I ask. I'm just stalling for time. I'm
just stalling. I'm just. I stare out the window. The trees have
red leaves shaped like hearts.

. . .

You ever laid your hand on a gorilla's chest? You ever felt the warmth of wiry hair, the roughness under your palm? Ever lain down with your brother, your ear listening to his heart beat?

The woman who came in from the cold

There is a woman we feel sorry for, whose husband wrote in his diary, 'Isla lacks animal warmth' and she looks at us girls, *Do I lack animal warmth?* and we don't know what to say and Isla picks up her baby and rocks him hard and we know something is not right and we say we'll be back tomorrow and we'll bring things for you, whatever you want we'll get it for you. And Isla says, she has all the things she needs but wants to talk about love and we say *whatever,* and then we leave her standing in the doorway, staring up at the darkening sky. All the way home we shiver at the predicament she's in because we know and she knows that when her man finally comes home, when she hears his motorbike roaring up the drive she won't have it out with him but will instead hand him the baby and say something absurd like a big wind blew in the night and she couldn't sleep. And though we don't know it yet Isla is reading about all the different types of love, *eros, agape, philia* and *storge* and soon she will put the baby to sleep and drag out the sheepskin hide and set it beside the fire. She will arrange herself naked on the fleece and wait for him; the wood ablaze all night, the window lit with an orange glow, her husband finally returning, his outstretched arms feeling the heat before he's even laid a hand on the door.

Russian letter 1

University of Kharkiv
1928

Greetings, Ilya Ivanov,
I want to offer my services to our glorious age of Science. It
is the only future I can see for myself.
I am twenty-two and in very good health. I am weary of
noisy high society and am happy to be in confinement.
I understand I do not have to see the orangutan. Or travel
to Havana. I read that science has a way of making a woman
pregnant even if she is unmarried. I hope the baby will be a
boy and go into the military.
I realise a humanzee will discredit the church but I do not
believe in God, just as he does not believe in me.
I understand I will be given more food. This could be sent to
my family address immediately. I am an educated woman as
was my mother, the ballroom poetess.
I want my life to be of use for our motherland. Please write
back to me. If I don't hear back within a month I will write
again as sometimes the post fails to deliver.
Yours sincerely,
Miss Maria Barskova

Russian letter 2

Podomosky
1928

Dearest Sister,
I know you will think me mad but after all that's happened
to me these past two years please try and be pleased, if
not a little proud of me. This will advance a great cause in
science. Stalin himself has given the approval to Ilya Ivanov.
It would be a huge breakthrough. There is no other way.
They have tried with the female apes in Guinea but nothing
happened. I know you will be imagining the worst. But just
to put your mind at rest – the orangutan will not be coming
to Podomosky. So don't imagine me at the kitchen sink,
the creature loping up behind me. Don't imagine a hairy
hand hard on the back of my neck as he bends me over.
Rid yourself at once of these feverish thoughts. This is the
glorious age of Russian science!

You ask if it worries me that the Church will be discredited.
What has the Church ever done for me? Our village has
been bled dry by the priests. You talk about the sanctity
of the body. My body is nothing but blood and bone and
empty spaces. More empty spaces than anything as the food
shortage here continues. Lastly you ask about the child. I
have seen drawings of what he might look like. You'll be

. . .

pleased to know he won't be as hairy as the orangutan ... and there won't be a long sweep of red hair under his arm. The military will train him and he will be of tremendous use as he can be out in all weathers, will be super strong and have no disinclination with food.

Have you seen or heard anything of Andre? I would not like him to labour under this news so if he or his family should ask tell them I have a mild case of tuberculosis and am in a sanatorium for nine months. No, perhaps it might be better to say, a year. Tell him I still go ice skating in the park.

Your loving sister, Maria

The birthday cake

The nurse said it was okay to bring in a birthday cake but not
to bring in a knife and *did I know where he was, had I been
told?* and I could see she wanted to educate me about matters
that I knew more about than her so I just said I'd be there by
two and she said *no knife, no candles,* and I agreed no knife, no
candles and on the way to the hospital I drove past a paddock
of horses, two of them were nuzzling by the fence, their big
bodies shuddering in the sun and I kept thinking of those
horses on the long drive, the way they communicated with just
the flick of an eye or a tremble of the lip and I looked down at
the birthday cake on the front seat and I laughed and this was
the first time I'd laughed for a while and by the time I got to
Ngawhatu I was ready to tell those doctors they'd got it wrong
and there was no point in putting him in isolation when what
would make him better was to touch another person but later
in that locked room when he put his hands around my throat
and asked if I was scared and I *was* scared and he said I'd have
to trust him and I said, wait, we have to eat the birthday cake
first, he rolled his eyes and grinned and we sat on the floor
on a rubber mattress, digging into the sticky cake with our
fingers and I was hoping like hell a nurse would be checking,
looking through the spyhole and later again on the drive home
I stopped in the fading light and went over to the fence and
I held out my palm with the last of the cake and I just stood
there and waited for the horses.

Father war

The war arrived in a taxi. As usual it wanted money, wanted the taxi driver to be paid. 'Hurry or I'll knock your block off,' said the war. My mother. Running through the forest, running for her small navy blue bag. The war. In a khaki great coat. Trying to grab us boys. My mother. Giving coins to the taxi driver. My mother. Pulling off her necklace. My mother. Pulling off her clothes. 'It's a game,' she cried. 'We'll hide in the forest.' Afterwards we let the war get lonely. We heard it play the accordion. 'That's better,' said my mother. Clink-clink went the bottles of beer. Us boys laughed. The war staggered into the bedroom. We threw our hats in the air.

THE HAPPY EGGS
FROM PODOMOSKY

Hot air

1.

The day we saw the hot air balloon sail over the nearby
fields, a sight which should have been uplifting, the
wheelchair man refused to go out onto the balcony, would
not join the throng of patients we carted, pushed, wheeled
out or held up to the big windows. So he missed seeing the
little man wave to us from his wicker basket, missed seeing
that glorious red orb sail out of view and we yelled at him, he
was daft, plain daft to wallow in misery when there were still
such wonders in the world.

2.

They said never turn your back on the wheelchair man.
For even a man with no legs could be a menace, could use
his powerful arms to spring from the chair and hurl you
to the ground, and this could happen while you had your
back turned, this while you were on the official business of
cleaning the ward, pulling your vacuum over the linoleum
floors, the other patients lying in their beds, except for the
wheelchair man, parked under the window, sun lighting his
unshaven face. Hot air too were the stories of how he lost
his legs; blown off in the war, run over by a tank, raging
diabetes, tumbling rocks, surging timber on the river and
more simply his mother's fault.

. . .

3.

'You girls,' he said, 'you girls can't take a bit of fun.'

4.

60   For all the times he'd leaned out of his wheelchair and yanked the vacuum cord free, for all the times he'd jabbed his finger at the floor, Here, girlie, you missed that spot, here you missed that dust, here you missed that glob of spit and us going around and around in circles but not ever having our backs to him while we pull the vacuum over the floor, for all those times including him refusing to marvel at the hot air balloon (which somehow changed everything) we grab his wheelchair and we spin him round and round, *wake up, wake up,* and all through the laughing and knocking into each other we smell his fury, his sweaty outrage. The other men in the ward, silent until now, clap and cheer.

5.

They said it was a good thing he'd been overturned. He'd been top dog in that ward for too long. But that night, when he quietly wheeled himself onto the balcony, used his powerful arms to gather speed, used his chair like a speeding bullet to hit the rail and sail over, those same people said we could have all been kinder, we didn't make allowances for his differences, he liked a laugh they said, him and his shenanigans and now he was gone, that wonderful wheelchair man.

Master key

The blue filing cabinet is locked. I want to get my life out of
the blue filing cabinet. There are records there: the children's
school reports, a pamphlet describing a colonoscopy
procedure, the sale papers of my mother's house – a photo
showing three hastily put up flower baskets over the balcony.
I ask my husband. 'Where is the key? The key to the blue
filing cabinet.'
He wanders off into the garden.
I find him stringing up beans on a bamboo pole, his hands
raised in the air.
He frowns. 'There is no blue filing cabinet,' he says.

Burning Faith

After the tourists leave and nobody wants to pay to see a fire-
breather on the street, I go back to working in the halfway
house. What the residents are half way to isn't clear but today
is Creative Therapy day and I've run out of glue for the
papier mâché so I tell them we'll be fire-eaters instead. We'll
start by putting a lighted match in our mouths. They'll need
to open up wide, otherwise they'll burn. It's science, I tell
them. Once they close their mouths the flame will go out.

The residents all sit around the big table so I can keep an
eye on them. And when one of the guys asks me how long
it would take to die if they swallowed a lighted match I tell
him not even to think about it. This exercise is a confidence
booster, I say. After swallowing fire, you can do anything.
That's when the new resident walks in.

Faith. She could be anybody's grandmother; wears thick
pantyhose the colour of mouse skin. She holds her head
erect and speaks in complete sentences but her hands and
feet constantly twitch under the table. Faith wants to please;
whatever therapy, whatever programme, whatever pill is
on offer, she will co-operate. So when it's her turn to put
the lighted match in her mouth, she obediently opens her
puckered lips. For a second her hand shakes. She winces,
tries to close her mouth over the burning match. 'Right

. . .

over, sweetheart,' I urge. 'Right over, until the flame's out.'
Someone else tugs my arm. They want to go onto the next
step, winding cotton wool around the fire wands and I get
distracted.

Later I see Faith at the sink swallowing water. The front of
her gingham blouse is wet. 'Are you okay?' I ask and she
nods. But I know she's not okay, she's probably got a blister
on her tongue and she's probably blaming herself, *stupid
Faith* but I don't say anything. 'Thank you,' she whispers.

And when a year later Faith runs out onto the road in her
nightie, flings herself in front of a cartage truck, everyone sits
in a circle and *shares* memories of her. One girl, still in her
pink pyjamas and Ugg boots, tells of her surprise when Faith
first walked into the house. She'd been her Bible teacher in
Year Nine and she thought if Miss Ewing was here with a
mental illness then anybody could get a mental illness. And
she felt less of a freak for that.

Then the staff tell their stories but when they turn to me
I don't say anything about the day we put matches in our
mouths. I close my eyes, remembering in my own way. Faith.
She holds the lighted match to her lips, thrusts it inside and
for a glorious second the roof of her mouth lights up like a
cathedral.

Born in the Year of the Horse

In the Boyang Gift Factory Yiwu watches the golden horses.
They come down the belt fifty at a time; heads raised as if an
open field might be just around the corner. Not all survive
the mix, the rough and tumble of the belt. Some pass by
with broken legs and once Yiwu grabbed a horse missing
both eyes and an ear. Very bad luck.

Yiwu eases off his face mask. Holds his breath against the
fumes. Gold glitter flies from his skin as he rubs his face. He
wishes he were back home with his wife, not stuck in the
gold room; thick gold splattered over the walls, gold globules
dripping off the windowsills, gold smeared over the floor. He
coughs, thumps his chest and reaches for another mask.

Before biking to the factory that morning, he'd told his
pregnant wife to be careful, not to place important furniture
in the northwest and south. Foo stared at him, her fingers
touching her swollen belly.

Idiot! You think I'm going to be shifting furniture?

Yiwu picks up his gold spray gun with both hands. The
horses need a final spray before moving onto the next
conveyor belt. He stands astride, sprays, once, twice, three
times for good luck. The horses rear back from the gold,

. . .

sticky blast. The mist slowly settles. Maybe if Yiwu had apologised to Foo, it would have been better. Maybe if he hadn't mentioned the furniture she might have waved goodbye to him at the window. Maybe the burning sensation in his throat was nothing. Yiwu bows to the last horse as it sails past.

Mr Eat-all

I keep a close eye on the circus man. He's the swallowing
type, got no regard for fishes, got no regard for other people's
feelings. I've seen him take two mice at a time in his mouth.
Mama smiles at him, shows all her pretty teeth.

He calls her mouth a sugar trap. He says he'll teach her to
swallow live frogs but Mama says the smell of frog is enough
to make her sick. Lately our mama retches too easily, she
can't eat her favourite; rack of beef, she can't eat nothing
green, she don't like food that's been pulled from the dirt.
We yell at her. 'How are you going to get us a daddy if you're
always sick?'

We bang our knives and forks on the table. 'We want a
daddy! We want a daddy!' Mama looks in the mirror, says
do we see a 'For Sale sign' on her forehead? Do all the birdies
stop singing when she sashays down the street?

'You not ugly,' we say.

Meanwhile we hide the knives and forks, the key and
lock. We flush the last goldfish down the toilet. 'I'm awful
hungry,' says the swallowing man.

He grows thinner. A lump bulges out his neck. He wants us

. . .

kids to feel it. 'Here,' he says, taking our hand and running it over the hard lump.

Our mama grows fatter. Her dress rips under the arm, the cloth stretches over her big belly. The swallowing man stands behind her. He proudly clears his throat.

'Can't we all just be happy?' he says.

Salt

Sometimes you can ask for something as small as salt only to be refused, the rules won't allow it. Then salt becomes a big thing in your mind and all you can think of is salt; how it's responsible for the salinity of the ocean, and then you imagine all the seas in the world, all the whales, then all the camel trains across deserts to bring salt to people like the big woman in the bed opposite. It puts it all into perspective when the nurse says, sorry no salt allowed on this ward.

You forgot to add salt is also helpful for mistakes.

Your father's warehouse begins to burn. Footwear and the inflammable mix of glue and cheap synthetic soles imported from China all go up in an explosive ball of fire. Salt could put that fire out. Your mother, on hearing the news, drives home fast through a blizzard of snow but the icy roads are causing the vehicle to skid dangerously. Salt could de-ice that road.

But all this is of no interest to the woman in the bed opposite. She's going on about her meal again; it needs salt and when the nurse tries to explain about the human heart the big woman raises herself up in the bed and says there's been a mistake, she shouldn't be in the cardio ward in the first place. She's only there because ward twelve was full.

The snake keeper would do whatever you told him to

… but otherwise he'd sit hunched in his army greatcoat reading a book inside the canteen. 'What about "enrichment",' we said, 'what about playing with the snakes or teaching them a few tricks?' The snake keeper raised his shaven head, stared at us. 'Now?' he said, 'You want me to do that right now?'

We called him Gogol. He never had any money, didn't contribute towards the flowers when Martha Worthington had her finger ripped off by a lemur and when it was his turn to bring a plate for someone's birthday he'd buy discount bags of potato crisps. The only time the snake keeper seemed enthusiastic was first thing in the morning unloading the truck. The dry food came in 40kg bags and needed moving into the containers by hand and he was always there before anyone else.

'What happy juice are you on?' we joked, watching him upend a bag into the emu tray. He was all muscle and lean grace, his hands a blur. But come lunchtime he'd flopped, sort of folded up inside himself reading a book or sitting motionless in the sun behind the canteen.

Resentment grew. The elephant keeper said he had a hundred times more shit to clean up in his enclosure than the snake keeper. The primate keeper reckoned it took him

. . .

most of the morning just cleaning and cutting up fruit and vegetables and why should the snake keeper have only a few live mice to let out into his enclosure?

72 We thought it was the snake keeper's reading material that made him the way he was. Russian books about war and exile and bitter feuding between neighbours. One day a few of us overpowered him. Threw his books to the chimps. Those chimps did a party whoop, tore up into the trees with them, hurling the pages across the compound.

Maybe if we'd left him, undisturbed in his own skin, the snake keeper would still be with us. When all's said and done he added something to our lives. Now all we've got is a growing pile of snake shit and Russian thoughts about how can a man be here one day and simply vanish the next.

The happy eggs from Podomosky

In Podomosky they run big chicken farms; each breed has its
own laying shed and inside every shed is an upright piano.
You can hear the plonkety plonk of keys as the chickens
leap on and off the piano; sometimes a chicken will walk
the entire length of the keyboard, other times the chickens
will alight at the far end tapping out a mournful sound.
Occasionally the chickens accidentally hit the right notes and
Oh can you wash your father's shirt, oh can you wash it clean? is
distinctly heard. Overall the Barnevelds are the easiest on the
ear, the White Leghorns the most raucous, the most likely to
drive a chicken farmer to drink or worse.

At night the chickens roost on the lid while the belly of the
piano sleeps. The south bound train to Kybovo roars past,
filling the air with flurries of snow, clamour and soot. The
chickens shuffle in unison, then quickly settle again, diving
their beaks under the purse of their wings. What is a train to
them when inside the shed is a piano?

The Podomosky chicken farmers have orders to clean the
pianos every Sunday. They use a toothbrush on the ebony
keys to dislodge grit and dander that fall from the chicken's
claws. The brass pedals are polished, the lid rubbed with wax
one hundred times. When agricultural visitors come from
overseas, in their long coats and stamping their boots, they

. . .

ask impossible questions. The chicken farmers turn their daft homely faces out over the fields. Light catches on the frozen stubble of wheat. 'Ah, so,' they say, 'ah, so.'

74 The chickens sit in their nesting boxes and wait. Their eyes are dark pools of happiness.

'And ye shall have dominion over the beasts of the field'

My aunt was Miss Nebraska 1963; way back in the days when the Meat Union sponsored the competition. The young women posed in tight trouser suits with half a meat carcass in their arms. They stood there, raw meat filling their nostrils, worrying the carcass might drip blood on their shoes. Behind them the loud speakers blared. *I love him, I love him, I love him / And where he goes I'll follow, I'll follow, I'll follow.*

My aunt said it did her head in having to cradle such a lump of meat for the time it took the judges to walk through the bull section and then the rodeo before mounting the stage to judge the finalists. She'd be thinking sweet and dirty thoughts involving her religious teacher. He'd surprise her from behind then next thing they'd be rolling around in a filthy haybarn. He'd slap her hard on the rump and she almost jumped on stage with the thought of it. She'd glance nervously at the other girls. All, in matching tan trouser suits, smiling over their carcass of meat. They were not like her. She imagined they had clean minds and wore clean underwear and stopped up their blood with tampons not bulky pads. Some of them tapped a foot to the music while keeping their upper bodies perfectly still.

When the judges finally assembled on stage my aunt

. . .

was ready for them. She hoisted the meat carcass a little higher up her shoulder. The surface was cool and fresh as a stranger's cheek. She let her lips part. She was a woman full of hunger and longing and she let the judges smell it on her. Later she would say it was instinct, she knew what those men, old and bald, were looking for, but later again she'd say that having the Miss Nebraska 1963 blue ribbon draped over her shoulders was well earned, and later again my aunt would say she could never face eating meat again. Or the religious teacher, for that matter.

Jesus and
the Ostriches

Jesus and the ostriches

1.

Soon after Roland began sleeping in the caravan I saw Jesus. He was just a shape at the bedroom door really and my first thought was that it was Roland so I lay there with my eyes shut. But when nothing happened I slid open one eye and that's when I noticed the figure had a thing on his head. A crown of thorns. A ray of moonlight played over the twisted wood. 'You've got the wrong room,' I wanted to say. 'The old woman's across the hallway.'

Roland's mother was always on about Jesus. 'He will guide us,' she said. When the first breeding pair of ostriches escaped through the wire fence and drowned in the river she said it was Jesus's way of warning us the fence needed to be higher. He warned us again when the chicks got diarrhea. All this Jesus talk didn't bother Roland. 'Can't you just ignore her?' he said, 'Can't you just do that for me, honey?'

When I think back to this, I should have tried to make things good again between Roland and me. Sometimes I'd imagine myself, crossing the yard naked, quietly slipping in through the caravan door. I'd pull back the bed covers and he'd wake to find me lying on top of him. But the thought of walking past the ostriches, lumped there in the yard, bare necks raised to the dark sky, kind of put me off. I'd only get

. . .

as far as the veranda before I'd turn back. Meanwhile his mother started pinning up encouraging notices around the house.

Each bird yields 30–35kg of low fat meat, 1–2 square metres of leather and 1–2kgs of feathers.

I said I didn't think there'd be any money in feathers but she said that's where I was wrong, hadn't I heard of the fancy plumed headdresses showgirls wore, hadn't I heard of the growing market? She said I had to forget about the setbacks, ostriches were the way forward and I should pull myself together.

But I'm getting ahead of myself here. After *he* visited I couldn't sleep for thinking about that beautiful crown of thorns. Then I heard the toilet flush and the sound of my mother-in-law's quick footsteps returning to her room. It was early morning; already the birds out grazing, the faint noise of tearing grass. I sat up. Jesus, I thought. I've seen Jesus. I walked into the kitchen. Roland and his mother were peering out the window at a male black on his knees, flapping his great wings in a rowing motion. 'That'll be the third time this morning,' she cried as he mounted a female. Roland turned. He waved his half-eaten toast at me. 'I'm ploughing all day,' he said. 'Maybe you could help out in the incubator shed …'

I looked at his mother, still staring out the window. She'd

been for an early morning swim, her wet grey hair loose over her shoulders. She yanked up the straps on her yellow swimsuit. 'I can do the trays myself.'

'No,' said Roland, 'you've got a bad scratch on your hand. Show her the scratch.'

'It's nothing …'

For some reason it annoyed me she wouldn't turn around so I told her the scratch would probably get infected … I'd heard a person could die from a bird scratch.

The old lady stiffened. 'You're talking before antibiotics,' she said, 'you're talking before 1940 …'

'No. I'm talking about tetanus.'

'Tetanus!' She turned towards Roland. 'Dear God, now she thinks I've got tetanus …'

That's when I left the kitchen. I didn't tell them I'd seen Jesus, I kept that to myself for quite a while.

2.
A hot wind blew over the plains and the distant hills browned. At night the irrigators sprayed water over the grass but it never seemed to be enough. Small bowls of dust formed, made worse by all the male ostriches fighting among

. . .

themselves. I watched them whirl and strike out, forward and down with their legs, their sharp nails slashing the air. When a defeated male pranced away, all bloodied legs and tattered plumage, I hammered on the window. 'Fucken stop that!' Meanwhile Roland went back and forth on the tractor pulling the plough behind. Doing his best to get the paddocks ready for the new birds but he was already a month behind schedule. The old lady told me not to worry. 'You're not up to working outside,' she said, 'you're better off inside.' So, I stayed in the cool house, away from the heat, the flies and the dull monotonous booming of the males. I sprawled out on the couch watching all the soaps on TV. Then just when I thought I'd die of boredom, Jesus visited again.

3.

It was the night of the storm and the old woman and I had settled down to watch a chainsaw massacre about a crippled killer. It was about the only horror movie left in the Video Ezy store she hadn't seen. 'You can tell that kid doesn't *really* belong in a wheelchair,' she complained, 'look at the way he's got his legs crossed.' I sat on the couch, spooning crumbs of chocolate fudge into my mouth. I'd beaten the fudge too long and it had already set in the pot. Now she was going on about how the kid couldn't possibly handle a chainsaw from his chair.

I scraped the spoon carefully around the metal sides. 'No one ever really knows what people are capable of.' The old lady leaned forward. She was working herself up to contradict me when a blast of wind caught the side of the house. 'Listen to that, will you,' she cried. She leapt up and peered out the door. 'Dear God, the caravan's rocking ...' she began. 'Poor Roland ...'

I put the pot down on the carpet. 'Well,' I said, 'God must want us to have a storm.'

She turned to face me, hands splayed on her scrawny hips. 'Listen to Lady Muck!' Then she began saying that she felt sorry for Roland, I wasn't a proper wife, there was something wrong with me, I ate too much, she was only living with us because without her the ostriches would go under ...

I let loose then. Kicked the pot of fudge so that crumbs went flying out over the carpet. I felt my spurs rise. 'Bugger you!' I screamed. 'You wouldn't know Jesus if you fell over him!'

Faith is to the human what sand is to the ostrich.

4.
I could hear her praying, a long distant mumble. My fists clenched as I thought of a throbbing chainsaw, a Mighty Mac chainsaw and all the terrible damage I could do with that. It was so real I felt the bed shake. The next thing I knew, someone was shining a torch in my eyes. Only it wasn't a torch it was Jesus. He wore the same glowing clothes as the picture in the old lady's room: a long white gown, a golden girdle and a pair of thonged sandals. His eyes bore

. . .

down at me, brown and huge like Bambi's. I wanted to say I thought you'd have eyes of fire … not Bambi eyes. Jesus raised his hand. His nails were very clean. 'Cleave to me,' he said, 'I am your true husband.' That's when I knew I wasn't in a dream, I didn't know that sort of old-fashioned language. I sat up, shading my eyes against the brilliant light. Jesus smiled. He placed his hands over his chest then slowly began pulling at the folds of his gown. He was about to show me his bleeding heart when there was a tap at the window.

I thought it was a branch, but no, there was Roland's pale face against the glass. I told him to go away, turned back to Jesus. The bleeding heart was surrounded by a little circle of thorns but the dark red organ was pumping vigorously. 'Cleave to me,' Jesus said again and put his hand on the bed cover. Roland knocked again. I couldn't believe the bad timing.

'Don't open that window,' said Jesus. He lifted up his gown to climb into bed and that's when I noticed his hairy brown legs. He's come as a man, I thought, not a god … that makes sense. He lay on his back for a while as if he were thinking. Then he turned towards me. The knocking at the window became furious. I leapt up and this time I screamed at Roland. 'Will you go away, damn you!'

5.
I had never screamed at Roland before. The only time I'd raised my voice was when he told me, just three days after

the wedding, that his mother would be living with us. 'She's got no one else,' he explained. I don't remember what I said, just the pained look on Roland's face. We were in the honeymoon suite at a Rotorua hotel, both wearing matching white bathrobes we'd found hanging behind the door. 'I want a harmonious life,' Roland said, tugging at his robe belt, 'I don't do fights.' I told him I was sorry – I wanted whatever he wanted and that made everything okay again.

I told all this to Jesus as he lay there. 'Sshh,' he said, rubbing his feet over mine. The room had darkened and I was thankful for that. I was one year off forty and already had quite a few moles on my stomach. I rubbed Jesus back with my feet. *A foot thing.* There was a long silence and then Jesus propped himself up on his elbow 'You do know what cleave means, don't you?'

6.
In the morning he was gone. There was a faint smell of his hair on the pillow – incense and what I imagined was camel. I felt sick and depraved. It was like waking from a dream where you have sex with your own mother. And the house was quiet, too quiet. I leapt naked out of bed and tore into the darkened yard. Suddenly I needed to be part of the world again … grass and dirt and sky. I went looking for the ostriches, found them near the shed, their bodies clumped together like a row of thatch. They stirred nervously as I approached. I came closer and I know this sounds funny but I felt if I could just connect with a living creature I

. . .

might steady myself, might come back to myself somehow. I reached out, tried to grab a female by the wing but she sprang lightly away. I followed. Tried backing her against the wire fence but she sidestepped and with a toss of her head shot past. Shit skidded down her leg. The other birds raised their necks in alarm. I watched the group whirl then flounce off down to the end of the yard. Then I sat down and wept. Not about the ostriches, but what was really troubling me. Jesus. I knew normal people didn't see Jesus.

I hugged my arms over my chest. Tried telling myself that everything would be okay, I could live with the fact that Jesus visited, in the same way as somebody lived with diabetes or one leg … it was nothing major and who would ever know anyway? All I needed to do was keep my mouth shut and not let anything slip, especially to Roland's mother. Life would go on. And that thought comforted me as I squatted there, digging my cold toes into a mound of dust and feathers.

As the ostrich when pursued hideth his head but forgetteth his body, so the fears of a coward expose him to danger.

7.

I watched the light creep over the top of the green caravan. A rooster crowed in the next paddock. Any time now Roland would emerge from the caravan in his blue checked shirt, holding onto his unzipped jeans. He'd take a leak under the gum tree before noticing me. He'd stand still, watching me for a second. 'Sweetheart?' Later his mother would arrive, running in her swimsuit as she tied back her hair. 'Come back into the house,' she'd say, 'let's get you back in the warmth …' But that didn't happen. No one came and after a while I walked back inside by myself. His mother had a towel around her shoulders and a telephone book open on her lap. Her mouth dropped open. I told her not to bother ringing anyone. 'There's someone else in my life,' I blurted out. 'So this is goodbye.' She jumped up, looking flustered but I pushed past her. I went down the hall, grabbed some clothes then threw open the door to the veranda. She came running and skidding behind. 'One day you'll have to stand before Jesus,' she cried. I laughed so hard I could hardly keep going through the blizzard, or was it a flurry swirling towards me … feathers … not the drabs or tail but white plumes rising and falling like a hundred chorus girls.

THE MAN WHO SAVED THE
WORLD GIVES THE TEACHINGS
OF THE TROLLEY BUS

I call my father Daddy and I know he likes that I do

… so I say it when we're having cocktails at Eddie's bar and he kisses me and says I'm the finest daughter ever and people only need to look at me and they know he must be a good man otherwise how would I end up the way I am, which is no convictions and manager of a hairdressing salon.

I cut my father's hair just the way he likes it. I colour the grey at his temples. 'Put your feet up, your head back, Daddy,' I say. He doesn't like 'palaver,' that is, a lot of talk about things he's not interested in, so I ask the girls not to mention the health-giving properties of the shampoo or anything about the Muslims next door. Keep the talk simple, I tell the girls, don't go loose with the mouth when my daddy's in the chair.

He tends to keep his eyes open when I streak the colour. 'Knock it on,' he says. Sometimes he calls the girls 'bunnies' and I have to shush him. I pull on his ear. 'That's no way to talk, Daddy.'

I walk him to the salon door. He waves goodbye, his hair shining with goodness. Says what he always says, *Don't cut loose from me, honey,* and then he walks off, his big, black, shiny shoes clacking along the pavement.

Babushkas

I don't have any need for a mirror. If I want to know what I look like I stare at my twin sister. Here she is, face tight with concentration as she cuts the throat of the pig; legs astride, she slits the belly and steaming entrails tumble out onto the snow. She kneels to pull out a bloody liver, announces there'll be a party tonight. Sister. I carry her inside me or is it me inside her, I don't know. 'What?' she says straightening up. She hands me the long-bladed knife.

'A party,' I repeat.

At first I watched her hairline. Was it thinning? Were the braids that wound around her head as thick as ever? I run my hands over my own head but fingers lie. I note the colour of her eyes. One day the whites have a yellowish tinge and I tell her to stand by the window. 'The window?' she says.

We eat meat every night until the pig is gone. Then Anichka from the far side of the Zone pulls out an accordion from her sack. My sister and I laugh to see her greasy hands slip over the box of wind. 'Stop it,' my sister says, doubling over. 'You stop it,' I tell her.

They say we are too old to worry about. They say our bones will glow in the dark. They say if we don't come out from the

. . .

Zone they will give us shovels to dig our own graves.

When we hear the trucks come back, the shouts of the soldiers, my sister looks at me. We have the same secret body, a ferment in our limbs, a ripening in our throats. No matter who falls first there will be no waste for the wind to pick over.

Madame Curie's swans

We think the neighbour's swans are quieter than ours. They arrived from Polska in the same delivery truck, were handled by the same workers in their biohazard suits but their swans scarcely make a noise. Whereas the swans we were given aren't happy in our flooded living room. They climb out of the water and onto the tops of the sofas. They hiss and honk and tug at each other's long necks until blood is drawn.

The children stay upstairs, peering down through the rails. The authorities have forwarded notices about how to explain the swans to the children. *God just made a little mistake. God just needs to borrow your living room for a little while. God needs everyone to make sacrifices.*

When the stench of swan poop becomes too much, the children hold handkerchiefs over their faces and try to sleep. It's a good time to clean the sluice gates, pull weeds from the water, do the radioactive recordings.

Late afternoon the swans seem to settle. First the big cob hops down from the sofa, stretches a webbed foot into the water. The female swans swing their long white necks around. Soon all the swans splash in. They glide serenely from one side of the living room to the other. When they open their beaks, it's as if they're singing to the whole world.

We wake the children. 'Remember this,' we say. 'Remember the lake, the swans singing.'

The mothers of the mothers of the mothers

She tells the child that if all the great grandmothers were
to climb out of the ground to drift through the cemetery,
it wouldn't be long before they came across each other,
laughing to see each other's old faces and say they were to
hold hands, the long line of them would reach the other
island, but they wouldn't complain that their feet were in
the cold salty ocean, in fact the mothers of the mothers of
the mothers were used to much worse, some having only a
potato to eat at night or soldiers burning down their whares
and others having to wear corsets of whale bones that go all
the way to their knees but the child says that's going too far
and she likes the part best where the mothers of the mothers
of the mothers wonder about the little girl who rides to
school in a car that does not eat hay but only drinks lakes
and lakes of petrol.

The General wants a new flag

The General thinks he has it all stitched up. Soon his new
flag will fly over both islands. He stares at himself in the
mirror. His chin has been slightly nicked while shaving. He
turns to present his good side, the heavy medals clanking
on his chest. 'At the end of the day ...' he begins. He tries
again this time from his speech notes. The words, Battle
of Chunuk Bair and Battle of the River Plate have been
underlined in red. 'Too much bloody red,' he murmurs.
The colour makes him uneasy. His new flag will be silver
and blue. His new flag will fly triumphant over land and
sea. Already the wave of support crashes around his shores,
already the rumble of stones courses through the streets.
One of the stones strikes the window. He peers out. Down
below is a great crowd. Rabble rousers! Some of them are in
wheelchairs. Some are old soldiers, some look hungry. 'What
do we want?' a loudspeaker blares. 'Food!' the people chant.
The General tightens his jacket. He leans over the parapet.
'My people,' he cries. 'Can't a man chew and walk at the
same time?' The crowd hurls their worn shoes at him. The
General retreats. He is the General of not one island but two,
yet at this very moment, glancing at himself in the mirror, he
sees only his nicked chin, the slight trickle of blood.

The man who saved the world gives the teachings of the trolley bus

Like many who came through the Cold War, Stanislav Petrov had his collar pulled up high to protect his neck and he was chain smoking. I pulled up my jacket collar too and would have lit a cigarette but the crowd at the bus stop suddenly surged forward. A trolley bus swept past full of tourists. The crowd fell back, grumbling into a queue. Stanislav ground out his ciggie stub under his shoe, calmly rolled another.

He must have known it was the wrong trolley bus. Just as he must have known that the missile alarms in the bunker that went off that fateful night were just a computer glitch. Not the Americans.

He could have panicked, pressed that great knob of a red button but he didn't.

I should say here old habits die hard. And nobody likes getting stared at, least of all in a bus queue. So that's how it was that Stanislav suddenly swung around to face me. A tobacco thread hung from his big white moustache. He thrust out his hand.

I was all bunched muscle and scared eyed. I didn't know whether to affect familiarity or pretend surprise at a stranger offering his hand. Over his shoulder I saw the next trolley bus

. . .

come closer. I looked at his double-breasted coat. I needed a double-breasted coat like that. 'You're a hero,' I stammered.

He laughed. 'Former hero.'

He had the smell of a man who knew how to duck and dive.

I told him I'd read about him in *Pravda*, I'd followed his story over the years and now, if it wasn't too impertinent, I had a question for him. At this the crowd pressed eagerly forward.

'I have a condition,' I began … 'a kind of wavering …'

'Ahh,' murmured the crowd.

Stanislav inclined his narrow head. 'And,' he prompted.

'I cannot make a simple decision.'

Just then we heard the horn of the trolley bus. The great rattle of wheels. Stanislav gripped me from behind, pushing me roughly onto the tracks.

As the big bus loomed over me, I heard him yell. 'Still having trouble deciding what to do, comrade?'

The blind heroine

When my eyes give out and I hope they don't give out when
I'm about to clamber down a rocky slope or I'm on stage
in the middle of a performance or walking past a burning
building just as a baby is tossed from the twelfth floor, when
my eyes give out I hope to have a dog that will lead me
around the rocks, skirting clear of the cliff and the play I am
in will be a Pinter where long pauses are to be expected and
where I will turn my blind face to the exit and slowly grope
my way out into the street where I smell smoke and hear
cries, running feet, and I stand there just as something above
comes whooshing towards me, just as something other than
my eyes urges me to hold out my arms, just as a naked baby
lands there in a waft of Johnson's baby powder.

Big Joe, walking on water

Because we wanted a miracle, like loaves and fishes and
because we wanted to believe that none of us would ever
die like fishes, our throats cut and our bloodied mouths still
gasping but wanted the other, going straight to heaven with
our mamas and daddas on the same golden path and because
they'd fired a monkey into space and it never came back
and because evolution was a story to scramble your brain,
because of all this, when Big Joe said he would walk on
water, would walk right across the lake on Sunday at
12 p.m. we said we would be there, *hell or high water* and
then we was kneeling down to inspect Big Joe's feet, his
splayed toes and his soles as pale as flounder and he was
saying he had to work himself up for the deed because he
was heavier than Jesus and because later when Big Joe was
tying a white scrap of cloth around his fat belly and the
wind was rippling the oily sheen of the water and the trees
waving around, we held our breaths, the gills of our throats,
until Big Joe steadied himself and began walking straight in
and held his big arms up high *Hallelujah*, and we all cried
Hallelujah, and we moved closer to the edge to see if it was
no trick and he really was going to walk on the water and
some of us saw Big Joe wading deeper, his stiff hair blowing
in the wind until he stumbled on something and down
under he slipped but others said that for a minute the waters
parted and Big Joe rose up, and there he was walking on

. . .

water, clear as day and because nobody was right and nobody was wrong but because *everybody* saw Big Joe climb out of the lake naked as an ape, and weeping, that is the thing we will remember most to our very last breaths.

The hearts of fishes

This day a widower man come into our schoolroom
carrying a fishing rod and says there's only one way to reel
in everlasting happiness. 'You know about hearts?' he says.
We know a lot about hearts. Look around and on every wall
there's sad-eyed Jesus opening his robes to touch a finger on
his red lozenge heart, Jesus, his organ bleeding and glowing
and throbbing and hurting and loving and sometimes hating
us with that wounded heart. The man points his fishing rod
to one of us. 'How many hearts you got, son?'

'We got one heart.'

The man nods. 'Here's the thing,' he says. 'A man got one
heart, same as Jesus.' He rubs his hand over his chest and the
gold ring on his finger winks at us. When the man's done
with his rubbing he says that when a fish gets a broken heart
it just grows another one. We stare at his chest, wondering
what's coming next. Suddenly the man leans forward, his eyes
bright. 'But listen here,' he says, 'God decided an octopus
got three hearts! Three hearts!' he cries. We start clapping.
Everyone is real happy for the octopus. We get so noisy Elder
Joseph comes in and as soon as we see him we go quiet.

And in that quiet some of us think the octopus must have
got three hearts for a reason and others think of all the blood

. . .

pumping through and how would the blood know which heart to go into and what say the blood went through the wrong heart and others again just stared at the fishing rod and wondered where the hook was because there's always a hook, you can't go catching fishes without a hook.

After the fishes

… we was hoping for another miracle, something that gave
us hope and then we heard our aunt was going to live in the
lakeside house and we was hoping it was the one who was
Miss Nebraska and stood on stage carrying half a dead cow
in her arms and we was hoping she was still pretty and would
teach us to drive and if we could of looked into the future we
might have said, don't come, but only Jesus knows the future
and he wasn't saying anything and so when we heard a jeep
heading towards the lake we ran off whooping through the
fields and there she was in cowboy boots and a black fringed
vest hauling long cases and camouflage cloth out the back
of the jeep and for a moment we thought she'd come to kill
ducks or swans but she lifted the rifles out and there was no
bolts in them and she laughed and asked us if we wanted
to be in a private army and we would be child soldiers with
real uniforms and black berets and if we did like we was
told we'd earn medals and money each week depending on
whether we was a private or corporal or sergeant major and
we screamed *yes!* so loud the lake shivered and a nesting
duck shot out of the flax, dragging a wing behind and that
was two miracles that day because then we knew she was
guarding eggs but our aunt wasn't much interested in ducks
guarding eggs, she lit a fag and hung out some clothes on
the line, black French knickers.

. . .

Straightaway we put our hands over our eyes. 'If you wanna be in my army, you gotta drop that shit,' she said so we took our hands away and acted like we saw and heard nothing and then she said she won a lot of money at the Casino and
that's how she could afford nice things and army stuff. 'I love y'all,' she said and her hands shook a bit as she lit another fag and looked over the lake and then over the fields to our place with all the buildings our fathers build and she said we'd have our own place, our own army barracks with a flag flying and there wouldn't be no men and she tapped the side of her nose and winked and if we hadn't of seen the rifles and the camouflage cloth coming out the back of the jeep we might of thought we was being tricked and later running home over the fields we suddenly stopped to make a circle, staring into each other's eyes, arms over each other's shoulders, hope opening out above us.

Must have been he wanted the lawnmower
to blow up

Our fathers blew everything up. They ran the generators too long, they forgot to put water in the truck radiators, they jammed the chainsaws in the trees and kept revving them. 'Run kids!' they yelled as trees toppled, as hot iron and sparks flew through the air.

The fields soon become long grass. We thought maybe we come from grass. They said we was Holy Seed. Some kids said it was a different seed that comes from our grandfathers but others said it was Holy Ghost stuff from Jesus.

We ran everywhere. Biddy-bid seed caught on our bare legs as we ran from the sleeping house, round the back of the church and up to the laundry where our mamas stoked the boiler and steam rose out their heads. 'We're hungry,' we cried. And when they knelt down, their sweaty faces smelling of iron and hot tubs, we didn't wait for them to say, 'Go to the kitchen, Worthy,' or 'Grace, you're too old to be running with boys,' or 'What did you do with the baby?' but we ran straight back over the field again, our quick legs swishing the grass, our mouths gulping the blue sky.

Our fathers said Deliverance Day was coming. They rubbed their big, scarred hands together. 'Time to build a space ship,' they said. They winked at each other. We ran off through the long grass.

The fish my father gave me

I drowned the fish even though I knew I was too old to be drowning a fish. It was as big as a real fish and I let it float for a while. My father stared into the bathtub. 'Sweet Jaysus,' he cried, 'did your mother teach you that?'

My father was a drunk, a dream, a chaser of women, a storyteller, he came from the Irish bog, his hat was riddled with bullet holes, he cried on Easter Sunday, got down on his hands and knees to look at a hedgehog, danced with my mother, smashed the shop window then stumbled home with a chocolate fish. 'You shall have a fishy on a little dishy,' he sang, opening his mouth so wide you could see the gleam of his gold tooth.

I cannot write about my father or if I do the story meanders, twists away from me in a slither. How can you nail a father down? Every goodbye was a wink and 'I'll come back with something for ye!'

The fish felt heavy in my palm. I traced my fingers over the ripples of chocolate skin, from the tail to the blunted snout. My father stood there, pleased with himself.

To drown a fish takes time. It tries to change shape, squeeze through your fingers. It muddies the bath water. It gets your parents talking.

Dirty mouth

I could always tell when the soap woman had been to our
house. For one thing, my father appeared brighter and when
he spoke it was proper and clean and not about shite hole,
scum bag, tommy rotter and up your coozie. *What other
clues were there?* A faint smell left on the kettle, around the
teacup where her soap hand had been. 'She ought to cut that
soap hand off,' I told my father. My father smoothed down
his hair. He eyed himself in the mirror. 'Don't go getting
yourself in a lather,' he said, 'it's only cleaning she does.'

Ah, but I knew otherwise. I'd seen her crouching down at
the cabinet maker's workshop. Her skirts tied up at her waist,
her lardy thighs on show. Running her slippery hand over
the runners of drawers to make them slide easy. I'd seen her
wrap her hand around a screw before drilling it in place, seen
her slide it inside a shoe to soften the heel, sigh as her hand
slipped inside a man's leather coat.

And now she was banging on our door again with her pale
lumpen hand.

'Is your ma in?' She swung her tin bucket in front of her.
'Only I'm not staying long.'

So typical, I thought. Full of slither and slather and quick

. . .

down the gurgler she goes. 'Don't be barmy,' I said. This is what Ma would have said and the words came easy. Behind me I could hear my father cursing about the terrible situation in the bathroom. I knew it was a ruse. They'd lock themselves in there. My father and the soap woman. She'd sit on his knee, lick his earlobes, wash his mouth out with that big creamy hand of hers. Later he would emerge, whistling loudly to throw us off the scent.

Ways in which I, Elena, never grew up

1.

I chase roosters. I like the weight of the warm bird in my
arms. 'Take roostie to the chopping block,' my mother says.
The rooster opens and closes its beak soundlessly. 'You take
him to the chopping block,' I say. 'You're the mother.'

2.

She left me too long in The Children's House. The high
stone building was surrounded by big trees and chickens that
ran wild down the backyard. The other kids all seemed to
have something wrong with them; a boy with a hare lip, his
handsome brother, Stefan who never talked but sat in the
dirt with the chickens, a deaf girl and a band of girls who
threw stones from high up in the trees.

I missed her. Once I saw her biking through the snow
towards the factory but even though I yelled out, *Mama!* and
she turned her head briefly, she went on biking.

When my mother finally came for me, I could hardly look at
her. 'Be careful of the feet,' she said as she lifted me onto the
bike. I sat stiffly in the little tin seat behind her. As she biked
past the gate I pummelled on her back for all the trouble
she'd caused me.

. . .

Now I yell at her. 'Talk proper English!'

3.
I do not speak to men in uniform. This has made it difficult for me when I'm alone in the hotel elevator with the porter.

4.
When I swim in the sea, I use a flotation ring, something to hang on to. I watch the heads bobbing around in the salty waves, watch children slip from their mother's grasp. I open my mouth wide, I am Jonah the whale. Under my great curved bones, lie a dormitory of children. I am always the heroine, the saviour.

5.
He brings me jelly snakes. I lie in the hotel bed stretching out the coloured snake until it becomes translucent, and sugary pieces fall over my face. While I'm eating I take instruction from him. There is so much I don't know.
For instance I learn about real snakes. Some lay eggs and abandon them and others give birth to baby snakes. We make up songs with terrible rhymes about snakes, screwing in lakes and jiving on cakes. He quietly closes the bathroom door so the guests in the next room can't hear.

One out of the hat

When Jimmy Clutterbuck comes into the office for the
pre-sentence report he brings his pregnant girlfriend and
a rabbit and I'm looking at the rabbit and thinking they'll
have enough on their hands with a baby let alone a hungry
rabbit hopping around and I know I should be looking up
the summary of facts but I'm mesmerised by the rabbit's pink
nostrils, all that damp quivering, the little gobbly mouth,
and now Jimmy saying he couldn't help himself, the pressure
was buildin' and the schoolgirl just happened to walk past
his car and if she hadn't of looked inside and if his trousers
hadn't of been half down and if he hadn't of parked where
he did it would of been all right and I look at his girlfriend,
her cotton frock straining against her belly and I say, I
thought all this would have stopped with you and she says
it's nothing to do with her and in the silence I reach out for
the rabbit, its paws scrabble the air but the girl holds on
tighter and in that flustered moment I tell Jimmy his report
isn't looking too good, he'd better prepare himself for what's
coming and his blue eyes open wide and he says he's already
written a letter to the judge about his new responsibilities;
father, husband and rabbit owner and his girlfriend smiles,
she has crack sores on her mouth and a bruise on her arm
but she smiles to hear Jimmy speak of her and later when
she lays out a stained tea towel on the floor and wraps up the
drowsy rabbit I think maybe – just for one moment – maybe

. . .

they will be okay and the bad report on Jimmy could simply vanish from my desk, in a sleight of hand so swift, we could all believe in miracles.

YOU ARE NEVER
COMPLETELY GONE

In the end days your father comes to visit

He wants a photograph of the baby in the bath. Or maybe
lying on a sheepskin rug. You say you haven't got a sheepskin
rug and the baby's already had a bath. Your father says, 'Well
make up your mind, sweetheart.' He wants a photograph of
his grandson before he gets back on the plane.

He picks the baby up, holds him by the window for a closer
look. 'There's nothing wrong with him,' he says. You point
to the baby's furry legs.

'It's nothing,' your father snorts. He declares the baby
perfectly normal. He unscrews the cap on the camera lens.

The baby, surprised by his own good fortune, kicks up a
storm back in the bath.

You lift him out, a soapy shawl of fur over his back. *Normal*
you say, *perfectly normal* as you wrap him in a towel. You
wipe soap off his developing moustache. Pat his legs and
arms dry. You wonder whether a hair dryer would be better.
But then you worry he might grab it, stick his little finger
into the whirring head.

The baby's warm fat body presses into your back as you jog
with him into the living room. Your father has already gone.
He has other grandchildren to photograph. Already they are
developing faster than he can ever record them.

Deadwood

We was tricked. We was told the sea was rising and unless
our fathers felled trees and built a boat we'd take on water
like a rotten pumpkin and then we'd drown. But what we
did was secretly throw rotten pumpkins into the sea and we
watched them froth and spin and sink only to bob up again
on another wave. 'Keep going,' we cried and we remembered
how we'd lain down with the pumpkins on our mama's porch
and this was before they settled and spread, this was when
they were firm and we pressed our cheeks to their thick iron-
grey skin and we stared up at the mountain and we thought
of bombs and radiation and all the things that could keel a
body right over.

Maybe if the adults let us look at the boat plans or explained
why the big waves was coming or why Elder Joseph took
the girl into the pumpkin field and she came home with a
terrible look in her eyes we would have known something.
But nobody was saying.

So we did our own trick. We said we was going to church
but we ran off to hide inside the trees. We breathed in their
good smell, rubbed together our woody elbows. When
light left the mountain we held our arms out to the sky and
waited for moths to settle on the knobs of our throats. We
thought we heard our fathers crash through the fields calling

. . .

our names, but maybe it was waves rolling shingle onto shore. We knew they would later sob, hold our mamas tight, loosening their long hair, rocking into them, this way and that and forgetting about us.

126

But we was wrong. The adults sung and hollered all night about the boat. Then our fathers was running towards the woods swinging their chainsaws. We poked our heads out from the leaves. 'It's us!' we cried, 'It's us!' but already our voices had turned to wind.

Who's in charge around here?

Miss Nebraska has a box of war medals. When we carry out a
mission or sometimes just march obediently around the lake
every day of the week with no one pushing or shoving and
all our rifles pointing the same way, we get a medal. First she
makes us stand to attention while she looks us over. *At ease,
soldiers.* We watch her take a medal from the tin box hoping
it might be the gold star with a ribbon bar of blue, white
and red. But today it's the round one with the King's head
so straightaway we salute and shout, 'God Save the King!'
It seems all day, we've been shouting, 'God Save the King.'
From first thing, when Miss Nebraska hoisted up the big
flag on top of the hut to coming to a halt on top of the hill
looking over the lake … 'God Save the King.' She holds the
medal up high. 'Which deservin' soldier is going to get this?'

Miss Nebraska lights a cigarette and tries to wave the smoke
away from us. She says she doesn't believe God is a man. And
when she salutes and says, 'God Save the King,' that's just
a figure of speech. Abel struts around with the new medal
on his army jacket. Later he'll be court martialed, the medal
unpinned from him but today he's walking in the sunshine
and Miss Nebraska under a tree drinking from her silver hip
flask and saying, 'Eat your heart out, city slickers.'

. . .

We break ranks and lie in the grass fingering our medals. The old war medals smell of blood and iron. 'God Save the King,' we murmur. When it grows dark we hear voices carried over the water, sometimes singing from the church, sometimes

the mothers calling from the kitchen, sometimes our fathers calling our names. To hear our name is a sudden pinprick to the heart. We like it but we don't like it either, the way it reels us in so that all we can do is rise from the grass and run, run for home, leaving Miss Nebraska, just a small figure, saluting us in the dark.

Man overboard

She met a man who made tiny sailing ships inside glass
bottles. He spoke reverently about the models on his shelf;
Santa Maria, *HMS Victory*, *Cutty Sark*. He liked her to watch
the raising of the sails. There was a lot of threading and
pulling to get the sails to unfurl. 'Let sheet fly,' he cried.

She clapped as the ship rose to full height in the bottle, the
white sails taut and spread. He laughed, drew her onto his
lap. His hands smelled of glue.

Sometimes she wondered why a grown man would want to
build such miniature things. 'Don't you want to travel?' she
said, 'Don't you want to broaden your horizons?' He slid his
hand up her skirt. 'For sure,' he said.

When he began painting sea scenes on a grain of rice she
refused to watch any more. She stood by the window, began
waving her arms. It wasn't exactly a Mayday, more of a pan-
pan; she wasn't sinking but she did need assistance.

Outside the wind had begun to pick up. A noise like the sea
roared through the trees. The house shook, the ships in the
bottles rose and fell.

You are never completely gone

If you get lost in the woods remember to hug the first tree
you see. Keep hugging the tree until your parents arrive.
They may take a while because they'll be busy collecting up
pieces of your clothing. Your jacket, your socks, your giraffe
onesie stuffed under your pillow.

The dogs will come.

Don't be afraid. No one is angry with you. Sing like a thrush,
open your mouth to the sky.

The dogs will come.

They will paw at the tree. *Where has she gone?* They will try
and climb the tree. Something has come up through the
roots, the trunk, the leaves.

Even the summer after your disappearance, the leaves will
still smell of you.

132

The Jumping Frenchmen of Maine
– the startle reflex

A river pig, you gotta leap fast from log to log, and it's
pile-ups, jams, getting caught between the crush of timber,
sucked under water, broken limbs and drowned and even at
day's end when you lie at rest watching the fire die down the
hypervigilant mind kicks in, a nervous tic, kick, writhe and
strike and if someone comes up behind, you startle, leap ten
feet in the air.

You look electrified, they say, marveling at the spectacle of you.

And if someone hands you a knife and urges you to throw it,
you automatically throw it. Smash the lamp is the next order,
kick the dog, slap the wife's face and you do that as well.

It's a syndrome, they say. Not your fault.

Your words are jammed. Somewhere between 'time for trees
to swim' and 'leather breeches to protect your knees' are a
dozen French phrases.

Somewhere in a doctor's office you bare your knees to a
rubber hammer. Your knee jerks up then falls.

You have an urge to drown the air with insults.

Father, mother on the cliff edge

My parents were sitting on top of a cliff when a young girl went missing at the beach. They weren't the sort of people to notice things and if they heard a strange cry they never raised their heads like some intelligent folk to remark, 'I think it's a bird ... a shag,' or 'Hang on, it must be a spoonbill, it's breeding season.' My mother would have noticed a fat person though. A fat lady in a tight swimsuit, or better, a fat person eating, stuffing their face as they waddled along the beach. *Would you look at that?*

I couldn't take my parents anywhere nice. I don't trust you, I told them, I don't trust what falls out of your mouth. My mother laughed. It made me happy to hear her laugh.

It was hot when the two policemen came out of the dunes and climbed the cliff towards them. My mother looked wildly from the flushed men to the busy beach below. A small tent had been set up and red tape cordoned off an area next to the rocks. They asked what my parents were doing up there. Their movements.

My mother said they were watching the sun go down. Watching the sun set, corrected my father. He made it sound as if they had some hand in this, some private knowledge about such things. Later they said they didn't know why they

. . .

had said what they did. They were taken by surprise, they said, put on the back foot with so many questions.

Soon after that my parents became invalids. *Invalids!* My mother began vomiting up strange little stones that resembled baby teeth. My father began to limp. He sat, gripping the edge of his bed. 'Which foot do I start off with?' he cried.

I read to them. I told them stories. 'You remember the time,' I said, 'I went missing at the beach?'

Are we there yet?

Don't ask me why, but I lay my head on the truck driver's
lap. Trusting he'll take me to some place pretty, not drop me
off at the roadside in the bitter rain. Down in the warmth it
smells of dust and tired crotch and diesel. He'll take one hand
off the wheel, run his fat palm over my silky hair and think,
What a little innocent, what a flutter thing that's landed here.

So, him driving long haul to Kaikoura, the meat carcasses
swinging in the cold unit behind, graunch of gears at the
uphill climb, radio playing, '*Love, love me do.*'

So, me thinking about the dead animals in the back and
needing proof that the night will give way to day and asking
him about his mother. She must have been a good woman.
And him laughing, saying he could get nasty talking about a
subject like that.

And that gives way to the flat plains and onto Cheviot,
sleepy little town, one neon light flashing over Rum Ray
hotel and no thought of running, not even then.

No thought of running when he pulls up at the hotel and
winks at pot-bellied Ray, that *yes I got a young sheila in
tow.* No thought of trying to beg my way out, avoid what's
coming because that bad thing's not going to happen. Trust
me, we're still heading for that pretty place … maybe sunny
Nelson. Maybe further.

The story inside her

There is a story inside her and it is about a story running for its life and in the story there are riflemen in blue breeches who cock their muskets and take aim. FIRE! shouts the captain. Gunpowder blasts the seat of the story's pants but the story keeps running over the marshy ground. All around other stories are running, dodging this way and that. Some stories fall like dying swans. Somewhere in the story she sees blasted feathers, and from a tree, a dangling participle. Where is the white flag in this story? Where are the stretcher boys to rescue the story? But oh, look – the story, the story that started it all keeps running. Now there are only ten of them left and the border is in sight. Hooray, they cry to each other. Hooray, keep going!

The story inside her says, that is your ending. But the story running for its life has its own ideas. The Captain must come back. He must tweak his magnificent moustache and declare something wise like, 'Do not hide your light under a bushel.' But who knows what a bushel is? Not the story running and not the little story inside her which is beginning to think that maybe that's where the story should safely remain.

NOTES AND ACKNOWLEDGEMENTS

The father of octopus wrestling and **Wrestling with the octopus**
These stories were inspired by a Wikipedia entry on octopus wrestling. I was intrigued to read of a man named O'Rourke who caught octopuses in the late 1940s, using his body as live bait. He was dubbed the 'father of octopus wrestling' by American writer H. Allen Smith.

Russian letter 1 and **Russian letter 2**
These letters were inspired after coming across several references to the humanzee files. The Moscow papers report Josef Stalin's interest in breeding a 'super warrior' from a human–ape hybrid. Ilya Ivanov was the biologist charged with this mission.

Jesus and the ostriches
'Faith is to the human what sand is to the ostrich' is a quote from comedian Lenny Bruce. 'As the ostrich when pursued hideth his head but forgetteth his body, so the fears of a coward expose him to danger' is attributed to Akhenaten, Pharaoh of the 18th Dynasty of Egypt.

The mothers of the mothers of the mothers
The bones of my great-great-great-grandmother Hinerangi Kotiro (1805–1859, Ngāti Ruanui) lie in the Christ Church cemetery, Russell, Bay of Islands.

The man who saved the world gives the teachings of the trolley bus
Stanislav Petrov became known as 'the man who saved the world' for his role in the nuclear false alarm incident of 1983.

After the fishes and **Who's in charge around here?**
These stories were inspired by the exploits of a legendary aunty.

The Jumping Frenchmen of Maine – the startle reflex
This syndrome is named after a group of 19th-century lumberjacks. It has been described as an uncontrollable 'jump' and/or sudden movements throughout the body.

ACKNOWLEDGEMENTS

Thanks to the supportive flash fiction community, my Ōtautahi writing group and writing friends, including Zoë Meager, Meg Pokrass, Leanne Radojkovich and Kerrin Sharpe, and special mention to Nicholas Williamson who has had to endure listening to multiple versions of the same story.

Thanks to Catherine Montgomery, publisher at Canterbury University Press. I am enormously grateful for her continued support and belief in my writing. Thanks also to Emma Neale for her excellent editorial advice. Finally, a big thank you to Aaron Beehre (book designer) and Katrina McCallum (editor at Canterbury University Press).

Special thanks to the Michael King Writers' Centre / University of Auckland Residency (2017) where many of these stories originated.

Grateful acknowledgement is made to the editors and publishers of the magazines and anthologies in which the following works first appeared: a version of **Seven starts to the man who loved trees** was published in *New Flash Fiction Review*, Issue 10 (2018); **The father of octopus wrestling** was previously published in *Connotation Press*, Issue IV, Volume X (2019); **The honking of ducks** was previously published in *Postcard Shorts* (2018); **The bride from Clarry's Vineyard** was previously published in *Landfall*, Issue 236 (2018); **How we occupy ourselves** was previously published in *Fictive Dream* (2018); a version of **The geography of a father** was published in the *New Zealand Listener* (January 2017); **There's no slowing down at Anne Frank's house** was previously published in *Flash Frontier*, Slow issue (2016); **A good match** was previously published in *takahē* 95 (April 2019); **Reading the signs** was previously published in *The Lobsters Run Free*, Bath Flash Fiction, Volume Two (Ad Hoc Fiction, 2017); **Keeping Evie Lu quiet** was previously published in *Flash Frontier*, Motel issue (September 2016); **The hairy child** was previously published in *Flash Frontier*, Tree issue (2017); a version of **When gorillas sleep** was published in *New Flash Fiction Review*, Issue 8 (2016); **The birthday cake** was previously published in *takahē* 95 (April 2019); **Father war** was previously published in *takahē* 95 (April 2019); **Burning Faith** was previously published in *A Box of Stars Beneath the Bed*: the 2016 National Flash Fiction Day Anthology; a version of **The happy eggs from Podomosky** was published in *Ripening*: the 2018 National Flash Fiction Day Anthology; **'And ye shall have dominion over the beasts of the field'** was previously published in *Flash Boulevard* (August 2018); a version of **Jesus and the ostriches** was published in *Phantom Bill Stickers Café Reader*, Volume 15 (2015); a version of **Babushkas** was published in *To Carry Her Home*, Bath Flash Fiction, Volume One (Ad Hoc Fiction, 2017); a version of **The mothers of the mothers of the mothers** was published in *Atlanta Review* (September 2017); **The General wants a new flag** was previously published in *Manifesto Aotearoa: 101 Political Poems* (Otago University Press, 2017); **Big Joe, walking on water** was previously published in *Connotation Press*, Issue IV, Volume X (March 2019); **The hearts of fishes** was previously published in *Things Left and Found by the Side of the Road*, Bath Flash Fiction, Volume Three (Ad Hoc Fiction, 2018); **The fish my father gave me** was previously published in *Atticus Review* (January 2019); **Dirty mouth** was previously published in *takahē* 95 (April 2019); a version of **One out of the hat** was published in *Flash Boulevard* (August 2018); a version of **In the end days your father comes to visit** was published *X-R-A-Y Literary Magazine*, Issue 9 (2018); **Deadwood** was previously published in *Atticus Review* (January 2019); **Man overboard** was previously published in *Turbine / Kapohau* (December 2018); **Father, mother on the cliff edge** was previously published in *takahē* 95 (April 2019); and **The story inside her** was previously published in *takahē* 95 (April 2019).